Tweenies™

That's My Picture!

BBC

One day, the Tweenies watched a video about animals.
"I'm going to paint a picture of my favourite animal," said Milo.
Judy put out the paint pots on the messy table and Milo
got ready to paint his picture.

"I'm going to paint a picture of a cat," he said.
Milo dipped his brush in the paint and made a big
circle for the cat's head.
Then he added the eyes,
ears and mouth, and
left it to dry.

Bella came along.

"Oh, a rabbit!" she said. "That's *my* favourite animal. But it needs a body!"

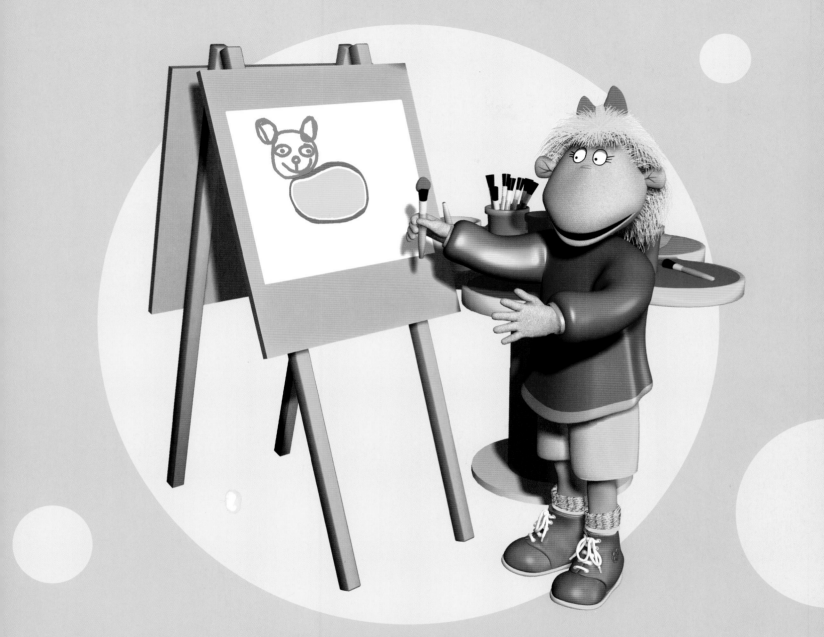

"I know," she said. "I'll finish the picture!" She picked
up the paintbrush, dipped it in the paint, and painted
the body of the rabbit. Bella left the painting to dry.

Later, Fizz walked past the messy table.

"Oh, look," she said. "A horse! That's my favourite animal. But it needs legs!"

"I know," she said. "I'll finish the picture!"
She picked up the paintbrush, dipped it in the paint, and painted the legs of the horse.
Fizz went to read a book while the paint dried.

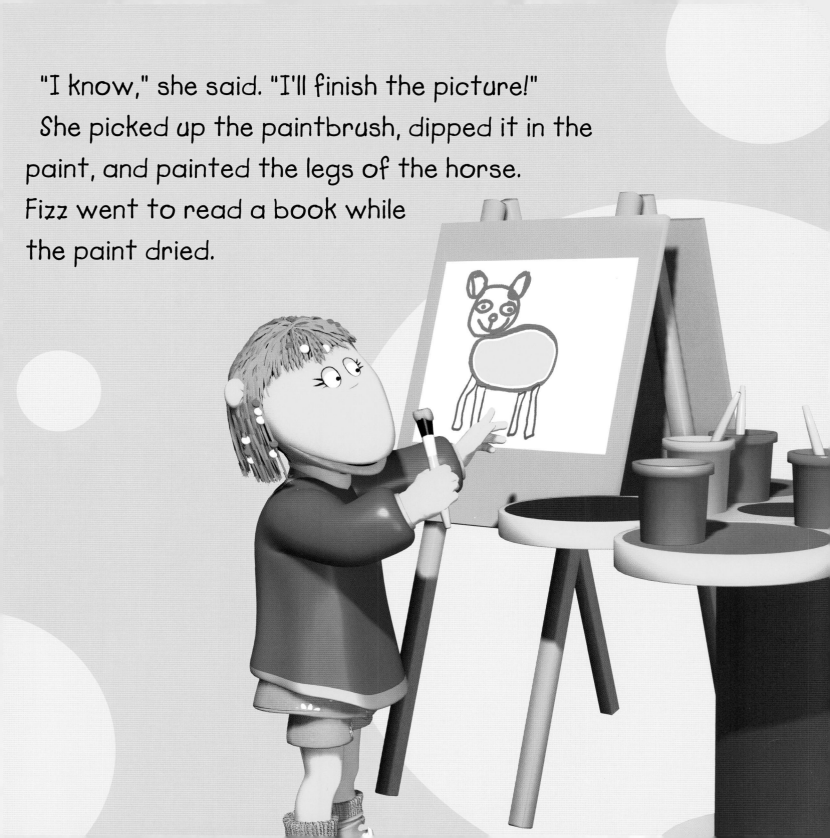

Then, along came Jake.
"Oh – a lovely picture of a zebra!
That's *my* favourite animal," said Jake.
"But it needs stripes!"

"I know," he said. "I'll finish the picture!" He picked up the brush, dipped it in the paint, and carefully painted the zebra's stripes.

Now all the Tweenies
had painted part of the
picture and everyone
had their own idea about
what animal it was.

As Max was walking
past the messy table,
he saw the picture.
"Oh, look at this.
A lovely painting of a
tiger," he said to himself.
"But it needs whiskers
and a tail!" Max picked
up the paintbrush and
quickly finished the
picture of the tiger.

Then he made a label for it. Max was so pleased with the painting, he stuck it onto a piece of card, put it in a frame and hung it on the wall so everyone could see it.

TIGER

When the Tweenies saw the picture they were very surprised.

"Hey, who's been messing around with my cat?" asked Milo.

"That's not a cat, it's supposed to be a rabbit," said Bella.

"No, it's not – it's my horse!" said Fizz, crossly. "At least it was a horse, until someone changed it."

"No, no. It's not a horse, it's my zebra," insisted Jake.

Max realized what had happened and explained that everyone thought it was something different, but now it was a tiger.

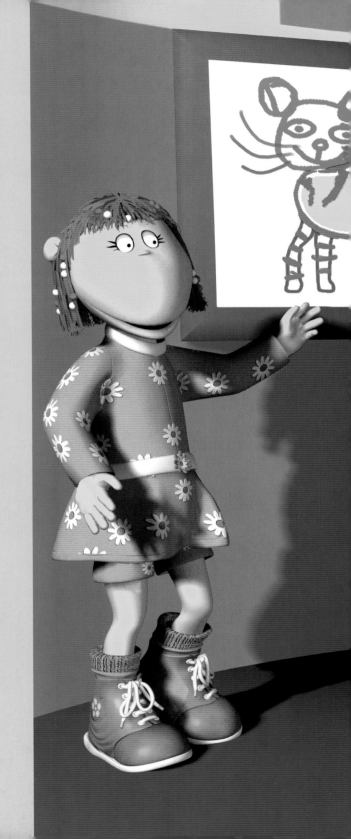

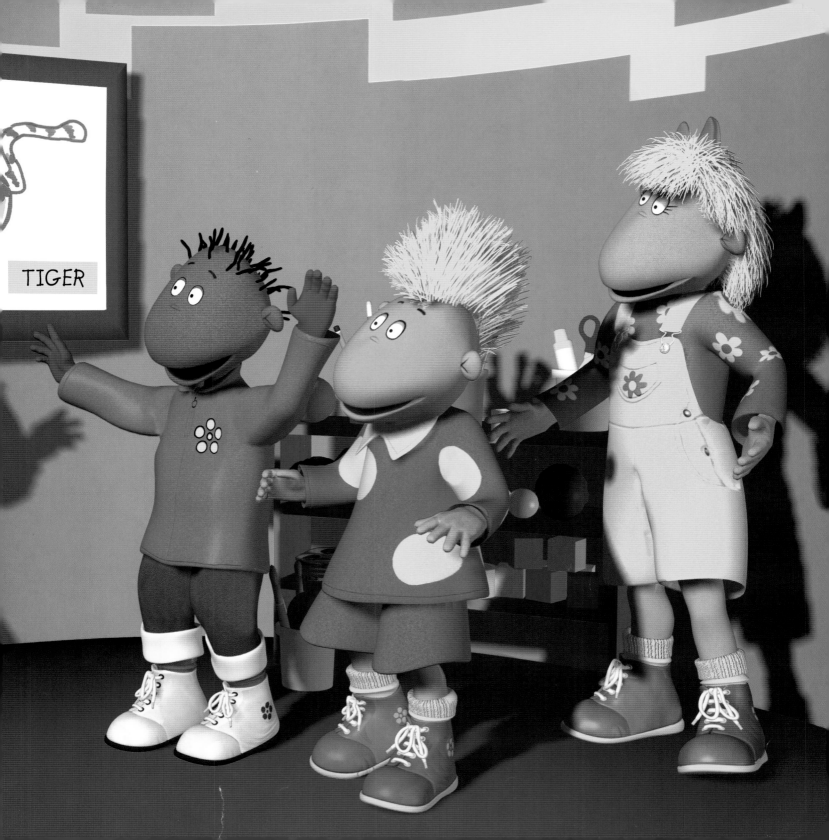

TIGER

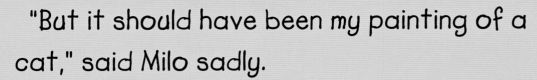

"But it should have been *my* painting of a cat," said Milo sadly.

"Well, a tiger is a kind of cat," explained Max.

"Is it? I didn't know that," said Jake.

"Great – I've always wanted a pet cat. Can we get a tiger, then?" asked Milo.

The Tweenies all agreed it would be fantastic to have a pet tiger. They decided to sing a song about tigers.

I wish I had a tiger,
He'd make a lovely pet.
If I could have an animal,
A tiger I would get.

Oh I wish I had a tiger,
I'd love to hear him roar.
I'd teach him how to count,
One, two, three, FOUR!

Oh if I had a tiger,
I'd take him for a walk.
He'd growl at all my friends and
I'd teach him how to talk.

I wish I had a tiger,
I'd stroke his furry head.
And when it's time for sleeping,
I'd tuck him up in bed.

So can we have a tiger?
You know it would be fun!
A tiger in the playroom,
A friend for everyone!

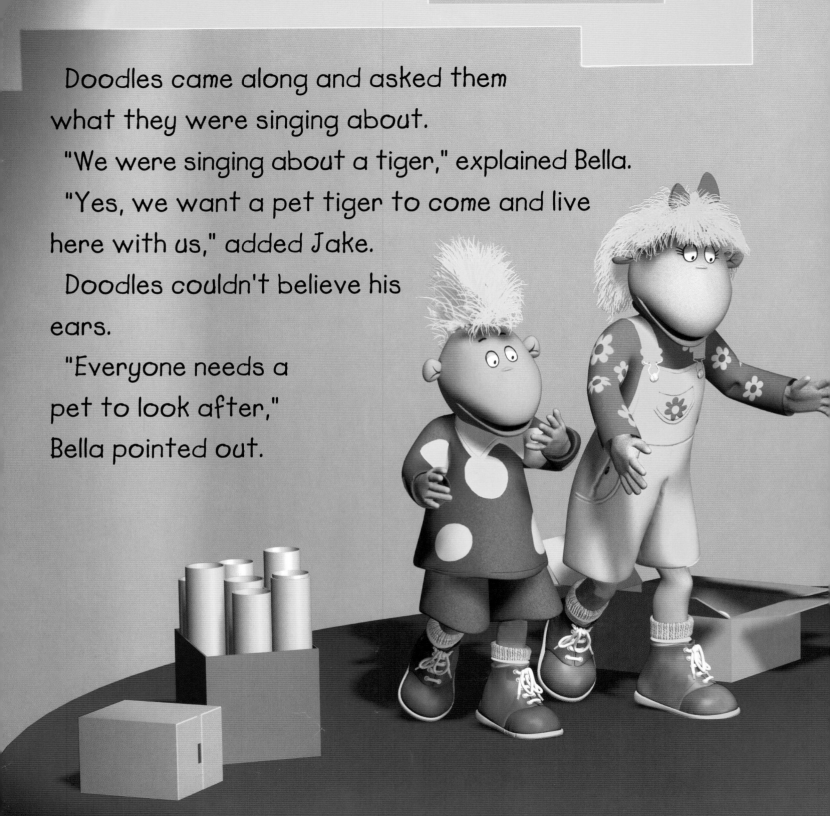

Doodles came along and asked them
what they were singing about.

"We were singing about a tiger," explained Bella.

"Yes, we want a pet tiger to come and live
here with us," added Jake.

Doodles couldn't believe his
ears.

"Everyone needs a
pet to look after,"
Bella pointed out.

"But you've got a pet, right here," he woofed.
"Don't you like me any more?"
"Oh, Doodles, of course we like you," said Fizz,
stroking his fluffy red and yellow coat.
"We just thought it would be fun to
have another pet,"
said Milo.

Max explained that tigers live in the jungle and not in houses.

"So, you see, everyone, we're really lucky to have Doodles. A tiger wouldn't be happy living here. Tigers don't make very good pets."

"No, they don't," agreed Doodles.

"Doodles belongs here with us," said Max. "And tigers belong in the jungle."

The Tweenies realized how lucky they were to have a
wonderful pet like shaggy, furry, fluffy, cuddly Doodles.

THE END